This book is dedicated to my husband Ben and grandson Toby and those friends who have assisted its composition by their encouragement and patience: and in particular to all the wonderful dogs whose names I have taken in vain.

L.G.

Contents

Dolly's New Home

I have a new Mummy and Daddy, it happened a few days ago…
I was lost, wet and very smelly just wandering to and fro.

They wrapped me in lovely warm towels after bathing me clean till I squeaked.
And my collar was thrown in the dustbin as I heard said, it totally reeked.

My new friends are Ollie and Teddy, Ollie is so old and wise…
Teddy's much younger and cheeky and they're a great couple of guys.

Teddy licked me and gave me a toy; he said I would feel more at home.
And Ollie said, 'Sleep in my bed,' you need to be cosy and warm.

I've got such a wonderful title…I'm now known as Dolly Daydream.
My name tag's all sparkly and new and I'm treated just like a Queen.

I know that I am very lucky… 'cos Aunty June keeps telling me so.
She's had lots and lots of doggies and lives at Grebe House you know.

We eat every day at three thirty and then down to the river we go.
And I bark 'cos I'm full of excitement when I see Ellie, Benji and Jo.

I'm kissed and cuddled so much now that my heart feels just like it will pop.
But the singing of 'Hello Dolly,' really just has to STOP.

New Friends

I am such a lucky bitch…I've been re-homed at the age of six.
My new housemates are quite posh, oh… but now I have to wash.
No longer do I look bedraggled, sodden, drenched or disheveled,
My make-over's now complete…pure luxury and such a treat.
I no longer resemble a derrière; I am a ravishing Border Terrier.

Teddy's a Lhasa Apso….whose favorite music is the Calypso.
He loves to dance and ruffle his tail… a very dominatrix male.
But he's so young at only three yet shows such pluck and bravery,
Like a sentinel in the hall… the guard and protector of us all.
So foppish and really quite a flirt, needing no lessons to assert.

Oliver….now he's a libertine, always one to contravene,
With deaf ears and rheumy eyes one can't help but sympathize.
He really doesn't look his age…that would be so hard to gauge.
Coming up to seventeen….. his muscles now hopelessly lean,
He's still a very noble Poodle whom Aunty June calls her Noodle Oodle.

Enough for now, but another day I'll tell you with who else I play.
There's Kuji, Ellie, Alfie and Jet, all new friends I've made and yet,
Teddy and Oliver are the best…A friendship that will manifest.

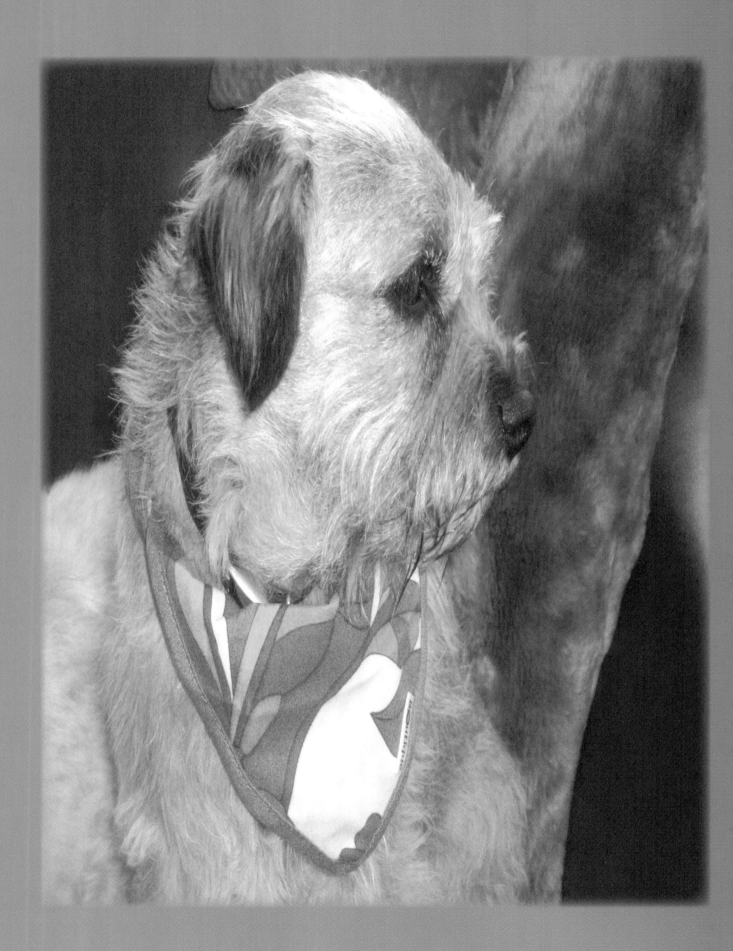

Dolly's Hair-Cut

The day has arrived as I knew that it would
And Teddy tells me that I have to be good.
I'm put in the car which I don't mind at all,
And harnessed and strapped in case I should fall.

The journey is great as I see all the sights,
'For sore eyes,' says Mummy turning on lights.
Ah! We are here, but I don't know where!
The Beauty Parlour, where they'll cut my hair.

The nice lady takes me from Mummy's sweet care
With instructions to clip here but not to clip there.
I'm having my bath now, such indignity
As I'm watched by that Spaniel and Highland Westie.

The drier's turned on so the work must commence.
The lady says, 'My, my, Dolly's coat is so dense.'
She clips and she clips to an inch of my life
All the time talking of trouble and strife.

At last I am done and she inspects my ruff
As I look round the floor, 'Is that all my fluff?'
Now Mummy is paying a vast sum I hear,
How fortunate it's only twice a year.

Teddy and Ollie, they say I'm resplendent,
Whatever that means...I just know I feel excellent.
Daddy says, 'Let's take a photo of Dolly
And while we're at it lets open some Bolli.'

Past Life

This is the third week in my lovely new home,
I've no inclination to venture or roam.
My past life was stressful... all barking and trauma,
The smallest gap in the fence was a beckon to wander.

I would scamper to where the badger sets are,
Just over the Lammas lands.... not very far.
I would dig round the sets, crazed and grazing my paws
Quite oblivious of any wildlife protection laws.

My coat was unkempt, dirty and a disgrace,
And I hung my head low from the whole populace.
Many times I was saved from wandering free,
Hearing, 'Poor little doggie.... is that a tick and a flea?'

Now I'm jaunty, sprightly and buoyantly sublime,
With a spring in my step I now play on cloud nine.
My new friend Alfie thinks I'm first rate,
In fact........ I think Alf would like a first date!

Oliver (The Dandy Poodle)

His feet are always manicured so never in the dirt.
He's slender, sleek and fit and can be quite a flirt.
With eyes so bright and sparkly he doesn't miss a trick,
Especially when the biscuit tin is opened just a click.

He's valiant and stubborn and fearlessly audacious…
With courage that can be heroically outrageous.
His intrepid escapades leave us struck with wonder,
(So why does he tremble at the sign of rumbling thunder?).

His favorite food to eat is unquestionably cheese,
I tell him if you go on like that you'll become obese,
Your coat will lose its gloss… developing lacklustre
Then we'll all mistake you for an old raggy duster!

He's now the alpha male of this shabby chic household
And must set examples too if I may be so bold.
Everybody loves him and just can't believe his age…
So I'll whisper seventeen and quietly turn the page.

Everyone knows Oliver he cannot be missed….
He's so adorable even strangers can get kissed,
Folk say, 'that's not Oliver…. he can't still be alive,'
He's so eminently glorious our hearts burst with pride.

Something's Not Right

It's two after midnight and something's not right,
Mummy senses it too and she's turned on the light.
It's Daddy, not well in the middle of the night,
He's shivering with cold and his face is so white.

The ambulance comes with lights all a flicker
To take our poor Daddy, he now looks much sicker.
I bark 'cos I'm upset, Mummy says, 'Don't bicker,
Just stay cool and relaxed – the sooner the quicker'.

Ollie sits next to me 'cos I'm sad and upset,
We don't know what's happening and Teddy does fret.
Mummy says she must go, should she ring for the Vet?
Though Daddy is sick other duties must be met.

We go back to bed to keep Daddy's place warm,
And I snuggle up to Ollie so I'll come to no harm.
Then I wake anxious in lieu of the calm….
Reflecting….. who will turn off the alarm?

Now the time it has come when I need to pee,
I start to fidget and squirm like an irritant flea.
Then we hear Aunty June, 'Are you coming with me'?
So we scamper downstairs brimming with glee.

The day was prolonged, intensive and drastic,
Ollie remonstrated that we must be optimistic.
I miss my Mummy; oh please come home quick
Now I'm feeling ravenous, frightened and sick.

The keys in the door 'Hello dears,' she sighed,
'I have to tell you that Daddy almost died….
But he's pulling through with medication applied.'
She was so overjoyed and ecstatic she cried.

Daddy is very sick with a thing called pneumonia
And her time spent at home will be somewhat irregular.
But Ollie who's wise and treats nothing with trivia
Re-assures me so well that I'm filled with euphoria.

Its one hour after lunch and something's not right,
Teddy senses it too and jumps from a great height.
It's Daddy…..he's home from his hospital plight
And he's looking much better in the broad daylight.

Our Toy Basket

This basket is chocker-block full of toys
With everything you could imagine.
There are balls, (one each for the boys),
But not one flipping thing with an engine.

Teddy would like a shiny red car.....
To set off from a chequered block.
He'd charge and race up and down the hall
Bumping into the grandfather clock.

Ollie has outgrown his toys too...
They just lie there all sad and chewed-up.
He used to love Daddy's old slippers...
But that was when he was a pup.

His soft animals sit so dejected,
Quite empty of life and stuffing.
That little black dog has seen better days
'Cos his ear needs a bit of a stitching.

As you know I like all things that squeak,
Mummy says I'm a 'Pip Squeak' myself.
Delving into the basket I look for my toy
But my favourite is up on the shelf.

It's my blue ball that's lost its entire squeak
'Cos I played with it rather a lot....
I chomped and gnawed till I ruined it,
Teddy says I have quite lost the plot.

I play with my chicken quite often,
Daddy bought it the week I arrived.
One day it got too close to the vacuum
Well, I just don't know how it survived.

Its poor little head got sucked right in
And the whole street heard my cries....
'Cos at the time the chicken was in my mouth!!
Mummy couldn't believe her eyes.

Bath-Time

The brushes and combs are laid out, the towels too,
Mummy's calling, 'Come on, come on you motley crew.'
Ollie doesn't mind he likes all the fuss and attention
But Ted is something else breaking with all convention.
We have the option who goes first (so we avert our gaze),
And Teddy's scarpered down the stairs ignoring Mummy's praise.

Ollie being quite a creep steps into Mummy's view,
'So you're first my little pet.' she quips, after so much ballyhoo.
We each have our own shampoo as we each have different fur,
They all yield lots of bubbles and sometimes our eyes do blur.
So we close our eyes tight shut wishing we could close our ears
For Mummy sings with all her might to allay our fears.

Ollie's looking beautiful... he's dancing to and fro,
He looks like an ad for Persil instead of a dirty yellow!
Mummy has to search the house for that dastardly Teddy,
He's hiding in the hallway...instead of upstairs getting ready.
The whole of our street can hear as he wails and has a good sob,
'Cos the brushing and drying of his tail is such an awful job.

Teddy's hopping round doing some sort of highland jig,
Now that he's been bathed he doesn't give a monkey's fig!
Strutting his stuff around the house, (he's such a maverick),
Swishing his tail arrogantly and giving a haughty flick.
Mummy's getting dry towels out so I know I have to go,
'Come on Dolly time to wash'...so I walk over kinda slow.

I have to have a special shampoo 'cos of my skin condition,
But I don't holler and shout like Teddy's sad rendition.
We have to leave the treatment on for a minute or two,
So Mummy sings yet *another* song.... of all the things to do!!!!
Once I am dry the showering's done and we can go and play....
But for our dear old Mummy it was hard work all the way.

Recycling Day

Its recycling day with boxes crammed to overflowing,
Teddy stops at each container the contents so alluring.
He's like a pig in clover as he sniffs each whiff and pong,
Mummy says he mustn't do it but he can see no wrong.

It takes us twice as long to do our business on a Monday,
Teddy has to taste the baked beans first at number thirty.
He's partial to the milk cartons which must taste very sour
And an age can pass if he should find a biscuit to devour.

Mummy pulls, tugs and yanks him but it's all to no avail
As each trace of someone's rubbish is for Teddy to inhale.
He looks at me as if to say, 'Come on Doll have a taste,'
But I don't want to smell other people's kitchen waste.

He pokes and prods the empty cans making such a racket
As he licks with great delight at that empty corned beef packet.
The trouble starts at number twenty, (as it always does)
Finding the empty wine bottles... for these he will not budge.

The Chardonnay and Merlot is in preference to the beer,
Should he lick Beaujolais you'll find him in good cheer.
Mummy's getting edgy and starts to continue walking
But still dear Teddy lingers with gait awkwardly dawdling.

Now comes the recycling cart.... it's making such a din
With bottles being smashed and cans squashed therein.
It clatters, clanks and rattles and scares Ollie half to death
As we try to walk away.... without smelling Teddy's breath!

Monday Morning

It's Monday morning 'cos the bed is stripped and airing
And Teddy's cross and out of sorts, enraged with nostrils flaring.
He's pacing up and down and going round and round the bed,
It's fairly disconcerting and quite filling me with dread.

But Ollie...curled upon the bedroom chair and yawning
Is giving me the lowdown on Ted's grizzling and moaning,
'It's really very simple Dolly... there are rules you see,
We always sleep till lunch-time... maybe even tea!'

Ollie's very elderly.... no longer in his prime
So I must listen to his words of wisdom so sublime.
He curls upon the chair, (such elegance adorning)...
Warning Ted and me to be quiet as mice all morning.

As Ollie continues with his house rule manifesto,
Mummy makes the bed with a flourish and 'Hey presto'
Saying, 'If you've sense Dolly you'll snuggle up to Ted,
Especially as it's raining and clean sheets are on the bed.'

So Ted and I go back to bed till lunch-time... I suppose.
We'll snore away the morning in undisturbed repose.
Just like our dear Ollie (who is now quietly sleeping).
Oblivious of any noise, even the blackbird cheeping.

I put my head on Teddy's chest as softly as I can
For I am feeling snug and warm in the safety of this clan.
The sound of Monday's cleaning emanates a distant hum
As I nuzzle up to Teddy... my new found brotherly chum.

Bad Intentions

I've just had my weekly shower......the medication stinks,
It's supposed to stop me scratching; I hope it will, methinks!
Now that I've been sanitised I feel like I'm newborn,
But Teddy's chasing after me with thoughts of doggie spawn.
My bouquet must be whiffy 'cos he wants to tease and flirt
Chasing me with bad intentions I must keep alert.
Mummy sees what he's doing and shouts at him to stop,
His ardour should be vanquished, ('cos he's had the chop)!

Can't he see I'm unimpressed and tired of his advances?
His come hither to me eyes and his wild calypso dances.
Any minute now I'll choke him half to death....
At least that's what I'm going to do if I can catch my breath.
Now he's been reprieved, 'cos he's been put in the garden,
Had a ticking off by Mum and told to beg my pardon.
Mummy says he must stay out until he mends his ways -
Knowing Teddy like we do it could take days and days!

I'll take this opportunity to read the *'Doggie News'*,
And catch up with the gossip from John o' Groats to Loos.....
An Alsatian with the name of Boris is working night and day
Helping to build an orangery with his owner Ray.
And a musical show in London with a variety of cats,
One is called Bustopher Jones, he's fat and wears white spats.
And dogs can now have passports to travel all the world
And breaking news at Crufts...as the winner is unfurled.

Now it's raining cats and dogs so Ted's allowed back in,
I've a good mind to be snappy but I'll take it on the chin!
He's looking very sorry and I really think he is...
So we'll get him a nice drink with just a hint of fizz.
Ollie has a word and makes things very clear,
'You can't chase dear Dolly.... permeating fear,
I must say I'm shocked that you don't show any sorrow
So I will teach you etiquette..... starting from tomorrow.'

Huffily Ted wanders off, (he smells Mum's blueberry pie),
Tail flicking to and fro................ and a mad glint in his eye!

Cousin Archie

Now I've been told I have a cousin and Archie is his name,
I anticipate my meeting him so we can have a game.
I'm told his pet sport is football; I like to play that too,
I have a ball that's set aside especially to chew.
His name is very masculine... I'm thinking movie star!
Or is he into music ....does he play guitar?

I hear he's hyper-active and drives everybody mad,
The milkman and the postman even the paper-lad.
When visitors call for tea it ends up on the floor
And Archie won't shut-up till they've been shown the door.
A fortune has been spent at canine behaviourists...
The last one was sent packing with two badly bitten wrists.

His coat is thick and curly whereas mine is very straight,
And we are both Terriers about the same in weight.
Whereas I'm a Border he's a Lakeland pedigree
And was purchased from a breeder somewhere in Dundee.
He likes to sit with his Mummy when she's finished work,
She has a very high powered job...from this she does not shirk.

But Archie hates her going to work and tries to bar her way,
He can't bear to be alone you see so causes disarray.
I'd love to meet dear Archie; I'd say, 'Dolly is my name,
What a pity you don't live near, it's such a crying shame
Us terriers should stick together that's the thing to do
Perhaps one day we will meet for biscuits and Typhoo.'

We'll exchange the gossip like all good cousins should
Whilst strolling side by side up to our ears in mud.
Then coming home to Mummy's casserole of chicken stew,
She says it's good for us and wards off the doggie flu.
And so I'll say goodbye for now, ta ra and toodle oo...
I haven't had my stew this week...Atchoo, Atchoo, Atchoo!!

Benji (The Beagle)

The name Benji creates a wry smile...
He's notoriously known for mile upon mile.
Nick-named Houdini 'cause he'd disappear,
Escaping his mistress for year after year.

He'd chase deer all morning on the Lammas land,
Then saunter over to the town's bandstand
And listen for a while if the band were playing
Then like a vagrant he'd carry on straying.

Going up Church Street to the Pepper-Pot...
Begging a drink from the shops when it's hot.
Then taking the path towards Catteshall lock
While trying to conquer his memory- block.

At the Boat-House he'd dally a while
Before heading home and that very last mile.
Most mornings we see him strolling along
His determined endurance still going strong..

Shuffling and ambling in a dreamy trance.
(The time this takes we could all fly to France).
Ted tries in vain to coax him in a game...
While I flatteringly flirt 'cos I have no shame!

He lumbers along....kind of dawdling and slow
Reaching the lock- gate it's ta ra.... cheerio.
I give him a kiss...telling him not to roam
But to have a nice day just staying at home.

Patch and Lola

Patch and Lola are elegant greyhounds
With who we like to have fun.
They run, spring and sprint along the river
Like bullets out of a gun.

Unlike Teddy who's an old lazy-bones
Or Ollie the noble laggard.
Mummy and Aunty Gwen reprimand us
For chasing the newborn Mallard.

Lola sashays like a model in Vogue...
With flair, style and panache.
But Patch likes to dig big cavernous holes
Then scampers off in a flash.

Gwen walks each day for mile upon mile
With her trusted companions...
Striding out with a passionate zeal
Then has to give in to her bunions.

Whipping up a storm of sand...
We dash and dart round Gwen's legs.
The swans and Canadian Geese take flight,
(As I step on the Mallard eggs).

We have such fun while Mummy chats
On the edge of the river-bank.
As I kiss and peck dear Patch's face
Whose nose is all clammy and dank.

But he gets annoyed, angry and snappy
If I do this for too long,
'Now don't get soppy Dolly dear,' he'll say
'But your breath.....it don't half pong!'

Molly

Molly belongs to young Eloise... (Such an exquisite name)
She's training for the arts and one day will find fame.

So while she learns these skills her Granny walks her pet,
But doesn't mind 'cos Molly's an endearing Collie ladette.

Her friends are Patch and Lola so it's at a nippy pace
As they pursue their quarry, maybe a pheasant brace?

Her legs are like the greyhounds, long and very supple,
It's Patch who's her soul-mate – they're a wilful couple.

They're shamefully defiant walking along the river-bank,
If they see a fisherman they'll wee right on his flank.

And salvaging his tackle... he'll shout, 'Oi watcha mate!'
And Molly had the nerve one day to eat his wriggly bait!

Granny blushes scarlet while she leaps to their defence,
Sounding like a barrister she pleads their innocence.

Dear Molly loves encircling us and kicking up her paws,
As we stand watching the canoeists paddling their oars.

On hearing a pheasant screech and take off to the sky,
Patch and Molly will scarper....... in the blinking of an eye.

Dolly's Itch

It started with a tiny itch and then just grew and grew
Until my skin was bleeding, from what? I had no clue.
In my past life it was normal for folk to misconstrue
Such signs of infestation which I must now eschew.

This condition went undiagnosed for age upon an age,
And still I itched and itched in a never-ending rage.
So I scratched that blighted itch.....my temper to assuage
As I thought I was the first to have the dreaded plague.

But I am getting better with help from Jane the Vet
She says, 'Its dermatitis....an allergy my pet,
I'll give a course of steroids... it will take time and yet
It will facilitate your itch so you'll no longer fret.'

Jane gave me an injection for worms and fleas and ticks,
And to be sure... a one week course of antibiotics.
Assuring me with correct use of dermal antiseptics
There should be no more need of vetinary medics

Now at this point in time I'm feeling fit and well.
My itch is quite sporadic....it will never fully quell.
I must not think negative but oh! that itch was hell,
Should that itch recur I'll yell and yell and yell!

The Four O'clock Club

This club is not for everyone... oh no dear not at all,
It's strictly members only and you must come with a ball.
You must have four good legs and a very long pedigree
And Charlie the Staffy is chairman of this canine menagerie.

They meet each day at four on Lindford village green,
Charlie is escorted there by charming Mummy Maureen.
She lets him off the leash, that's when he takes command,
'Now who's turned up today, who's in my little band?'

The Terriers are signing in, there's my cousin I can see...
He plays football very well yes, its good-looking Archie,
Here comes lovely Wheaten Lola (she's good for a laugh),
She kicks a ball like Kevin Keegan, she don't do things by half.

Millie the Snauzer's arrived; she's such a pretty bitch,
She plays with silly sticks but, please not on the football pitch.
This can't be Bulldog Poppy; she finds it difficult to attend
Always wanting to change the rules, modify and amend.

But today it's the Annual Meeting so everyone's here in force,
There'll be no games of ball or sticks - that's all in due course.
Now here comes Prissy Missy the chairman's bit of fluff,
She's always late, no-one cares 'cos Charlie might get rough.

Now Charlie stamps his paws to start the proceedings,
'Is there anyone here today to challenge my managings?'
The green is hushed and quiet, not a whimper is imparted
'Settled then,' says Charlie 'Is that Archie who just farted?'

And so for another year dear Charlie will take the chair,
He'll officiate the disagreements and at all times be fair.
So let the games commence ...'Now Pip no need to shout,
The ball...it was offside... don't argue, I say you're OUT!!!'

Ellie (The Giant Poodle)

Ellie lives next door to us with our dear Aunty June,
She's a giant Poodle.... as dark as a dried prune.
'Dear Ellie' as she's known is fabulously chic,
She's absolutely beautiful and oh so magnifique.
Like a gigantic mammoth she towers over me,
It's like an April shower when she cocks her leg to pee.

We see her on our walks almost every single day....
Unlike many of our friends Ellie's never a lot to say.
She doesn't like to gossip or dish the canine dirt...
Not even a wink or even a blink and never ever a flirt.
I'd like to know her better but can't see a mutual spark
Or anything convivial and I've never heard her bark!

The squirrels in her garden drive her mad as a March hare
While the pheasants swoop and dive in a game of dare.
There's always tasty bird food just inside their gate,
And my paw can just fit through if I wriggle and gyrate.
Dear Ellie stands at the kitchen sink observing what I do,
As she does the dishes..... she'll sometimes bark, 'Oi you!'

Disraeli

I have just met... Disraeli the Pug,
Whose face is akin to a black wrinkly slug.
Some turn away with a nonchalant shrug
Not me....I just wanted a squeeze and bear- hug.

He lazes all day on a red Persian rug
Drinking pink champagne (the very best Krug).
He swigs it all down with a guzzling glug...
From his Minton bone china gold plated jug.

He stumbles into a dark boozy fug
But sleeping it off in an old garden trug...
He's nibbled and gnawed by a great stinging bug
And the bite is now prickling his black wrinkly mug.

Declaring the bug is an eight –legged thug...
He's obsessed with filling all holes with a plug,
Then he soothed his bite with a comforting drug,
The stronger the better for this little pug.

My Best Friend

Kuji's my best friend....
She's good-looking and a dear,
Her coat's soft like plush velvet
Resembling pure cashmere.
Appealingly good looking from
Her head down to her feet....
As she totters up and down
And all along our street.

Now she visits experts...
Who groom and gently tease
Her hair that is so lustrous
To float in the soft breeze.
Ted and Ollie fawn and flirt
Embarrassingly so.
I don't know where to put my face,
So I watch a big black crow.

She has a little problem
With health says our good source,
Not all the time but now and then
She's not par for the course.
This saddens all who love her
With such regret and sorrow,
We'll send a little 'Get Well' card
To reach her by tomorrow.

We meet at half past eight
And then again at four.
Sometimes we see a pheasant,
A grouse or a jackdaw.
We always see dear Ellie
At the goblins pool.....
Where we stop to paddle
And nonchalantly cool.

Kuji's lovely Mummy Jude
Does Yoga to stay trim.
She's the envy of the tow-path
As she's diminutively slim.
Her forte lies in cooking
Scrumptious, yummy strawberry tarts
And chooses to ignore
Weight Watcher's diet charts.

We see them in all weathers...
When the skies are blue and clear,
Or when the wind blows in our faces
Bringing a stinging tear.
With snow covering the ground
And Jack Frost nipping my nose.
Or walking through the heather...
(That's in Springtime I suppose).

In the summer...I hope my friend
Will come to stay,
We'll amuse ourselves with games
And walk along the river Wey.
Have Jaffa cakes for tea....
Of which we're all quite partial,
If Ted can reach the china now
We'll have a quick rehearsal.

A Lot of Weather

The weather is ghastly...coming in from the Irish coast.
'Storms will batter England,' (so says the Morning Post).
Rain splatters at the windows making a deafening sound
And the wind is gusting gale force...... I'll be bound!

Sand-bags are distributed as the river's high to-day,
With coasts on flood alert.....surprising for the month of May.
The garden is awash with blossom and debris from the trees
And we're a little worried now about our hive of bees.

Wearing our winter coats, mine is waxed and smart....
Ollie's in pillar-box red.... but Ted says I look a tart!
He's being vindictive, 'cos he didn't sleep to-day,
Aunty June says I look very chic and Ted's got too much to say.

Our walk is so eventful, when unleashed I'm blown away.
It's Mr McCann who saves me from the river Wey.
'Oh, my Dolly', Mummy weeps......her lashes all a flutter,
Seeking to impress Mr McCann with a voice as soft as butter.

The sign on the lock-gate reads, 'Closed due to bad weather,'
And everyone's wearing wellies and mucking- in together.
The owners of the narrow boats doubt if they'll stay afloat,
And the cows in the adjacent field are surrounded by a moat.

We brave this state of affairs to return home to sit out the storm,
Making buttery crumpets for tea; and getting back to some norm.
Maybe we'll watch England play cricket...in Aussie where it's hot
And imagine we've won the toss and the Ashes in the little pot.

Kerbside

We're standing on the kerbside
Trying to cross this bloody road.
I don't mean to swear but,
To-day there's a squashed toad.
It's the same every morning
As we stand rooted to this spot
Just when we think it's safe
There comes another lot.

Now we've got a Sainsbury's
In this town of Godalming.
Homebase and Waitrose
It's great for our shopping.
They're just around the corner
From this bloody road.
Now here comes another
With a cryogenic load.

All we want to do
Is cross to that bit of marsh,
Do our piddles and poos
Without horns being too harsh.
We've tried to go halfway,
But we thought the end was nigh
When a doddery old fart yelled
'Do you lot want to die'?

Here we stand like lemmings
About to end it all.
Not a truck or car will stop,
Nor white van for a brawl.
Now there seems to be a lull,
Shall we take a chance?
On this bloody road there's
No time for dalliance.

On the other side
There's debris all around.
Hub caps here, reflectors there
A horn that doesn't sound.
And a medic centre stands
On this bloody road...
Just in case we all end up
Like that little Toad.

The Garden

I'm sitting in our garden by the Jacaranda tree...
Watching next door's Persian cat... old Montgomery.
Teddy's chasing baby frogs just by the water barrel,
And Mummy's pootling about in her old gardening apparel...
Wearing a frivolous hat to protect her bleach blond hair
In a get-up that's uncommon to her usual style and flair.

I like to accompany Mummy nurturing this patio plot...
As she tells me all about the plants in this her Camelot.
Muttering as she wanders from shrub to climbing rose,
Secateurs at the ready... she fastidiously weeds and hoes.
'The Clematis Montana needs a prune', she'll say to me,
(I don't know how she'll manage that...its half way up a tree)!

She watches Alan Titchmarsh and sometimes Monty Don...
Taking their advice from shows at Chelsea and Hampton.
The garden's in abundance with flowering displays
But also leafy shelter from the harmful mid-day rays.
That's where you'll find dear Ollie...under the Canary Rose,
Away from any chaos he'll relax and sometimes doze.

The snails have all been slaughtered so the Hosta's can survive
And how she does it, I don't know... she picks the slugs up live.
The Tree Fern's been unwrapped... from its winter straw
And is now considerably impeding the path to the front door.
She says it is an errant ploy to keep the post at bay...
(If it can't reach the front door... they'll be no bills to pay)!!

She'll 'pop down' to the nursery for a bag of bark chippings
And come back three hours later with plans for designing's!!!
Last week she made a rock garden within a kitchen sink...
Planting it with Alyssum and Dianthus 'Pikes Pink'.
Should a rose show signs of sticky aphids or greenfly....
The Bug-Gun will appear and the poor mites have to die.

Old (fat) Montgomery and I are keen fanatical foes...
Since he crept into the garden and dug up a prize rose.
We've had many a spit and a spat outside of our back-door
Causing the neighbours to call... when they hear such uproar.
But to-day is too darn hot for a commotion or a tussle...
So we'll ignore old (fat) Monty... who's threatening a kerfuffle.

Thus I'm sitting in the garden by the Jacaranda tree...
Watching the fluttering of a Robin and a pollinating bee.
Ted's given up his chase and is snoring by the shed...
Dreaming of frog's legs in garlic... on a lettuce bed.
Whilst Mummy says she's, 'popping out' (just for a little while),
There's an offer at the nursery on aromatic Chamomile!!!

It's Cold

I'm sitting in the downstairs loo,
'Tis the warmest place to be.
It being the smallest room
There's just enough span for me.

It's all to do with this global warming,
This unseasonable weather,
I heard my Mummy speak of this
She's so terribly clever.

We have to go out early morning,
Such a shock when we step out the door.
The frost makes us all a bit nippy
'Cos we want to be warm as before.

Ted walks pressed up close to Ollie
To keep me in the middle like toast,
And Mummy says, 'We're so very lucky
As it's much colder down on the coast.'

So here I am in the loo.......
'Cos the pipes are so cosy and warm.
It will be below freezing all day,
The thought does imbue such alarm.

So I'll just stay here in the loo.....
Dreaming of chilling all day,
Under a coconut palm
In a secluded Jamaican bay.

Daisy

Daisy is a little Jack Russell (and belongs to a lady called Di)
She's just a few months old... so a wee bit timid and shy.
She mixes in very high circles in a place called Manor Mead,
A home for retired clergy of the Christian creed.

She wears a lovely red collar but recently strayed and got lost,
But one of the Canons found her just before Pentecost.
The Canon was getting ready for the Eucharist prayers
When he espied little Daisy...there at the foot of the stairs.

She was disoriented and in very great need
Of kindness and understanding, (and of course her red tartan lead).
Forgetting his scheduled agenda the Canon picked Daisy up
And tears came to his eyes as he cradled this little pup.

Reminiscent of long ago when he was just a lad...
On entering his calling he renounced his Jack, (Galahad).
Now everything's tickity boo in this ecclesiastical home,
All peace and serenity 'cos Daisy doth no longer roam.

She walks alongside Di who's a nurse at Manor Mead
Caring for the elderly clergy of the Christian creed.
When Daisy spots the Canon (so gentle in his ways)
She's reminded of his kindness and for a moment stays.

His memories take him back, as he cleans the silver chalice
To when he was a choirboy with his thoughts of saintly pious.
And Galahad at the altar, (appearing slightly bored)
Mindful of his master whom he worshipped and adored.

Now Daisy's doing a Pat Dog job down at Manor Mead,
Bringing delight and joy and such happiness indeed.
She met His Grace the Archbishop not so very long ago
And in awe and jubilation felt a holy inner glow.

When prayers are read at Mass she sits at the chapel door
Enraptured by the hymns and of course psalm twenty four.
All Things Bright and Beautiful brings a glint into her eye
As she prays she can live here till the day that she doth die.

Where's My Blue Ball

Who's got my blue ball? I'm looking everywhere,
Under the table and behind the spoon-back chair.
Could it be up-stairs on the very last tread?
Or in the bedroom hiding under Mummy's bed.

I'm finding lots of dust and it's all going up my nose,
It's not been vacuumed for Oh! Heaven knows.
Mummy's far too busy she's writing a book
About God knows what (I hope how to cook)?

The conservatory was where I saw it last...
When Mummy had a guest from her adolescent past.
They had tea in fancy china, so my ball was confiscated
As they sipped earl grey and on biscuits masticated.

You think I'm making quite a fuss and a kerfuffle
Over a ball that doesn't squeak and has a noiseless muffle.
I can't ask help from Teddy, he's upstairs fast asleep,
His nose is twitching madly that means he's counting sheep.

I'm rummaging around down the side of the settee...
Could it be here with the crumbs from last night's tea?
Now the front door opens and Grandma's come for lunch,
She's arrived too early, (so Mummy's making brunch).

I can smell the sausages sizzling in the pan...
And Grandma's chatting on about the fashions in Milan.
No-one seems to care that I'm in a distressed state,
So I'll take another look in the glass recycling crate.

I cannot think where else to look and I'm about to cry,
Please... nobody talk to me or I'll curl up and die!
'Oh, hello Dolly, I didn't see you there...
Move your ball dear and I'll sit in that chair'.

Our Mummy

Mummy's hearing aid is kaput, so we have to bark and holler
And her false eye's on the blink which is such an awful bother.
She needs a dental bridge and a new porcelain crown
And her knees go click and clack when she is bending down.

When young she was a beauty, (Yes, a Beauty Queen),
And modelled for Norman Hartnell in gowns of mauve and green.
She was so young and slender.... a willowy size ten,
But this is present day Mummy and that was then.

When did she get these wrinkles she sees before her now?
And these worried lines across her rutted, furrowed brow.
Her hair was always bouffanted at a London Salon...
Now it's done by a young kid..... known only as Sharon.

She used to dance till dawn in her winkle-picker shoes,
Down at Ronnie Scott's swinging to the jazzy blues.
Or perchance Rudolph Nureyev..... At the Royal Ballet
(Of course evening performance...not the matinee).

She's eaten caviar at a little bistro cafe,
While sheltering from soft rain on the Champs Elysee.
Then cruising down the Seine on some romantic jaunt
In the latest nautical fashions...... (By Mary Quant).

She's dined at The White Elephant and drank at The Savoy,
Driven in limousines and played roulette at The Playboy.
Holidayed in Marbella, Rome and along the Cote d Azur,
Had gifts of gold and diamonds and exotic scented myrrh.

Her beau's were few and far between (in fact hardly any)
For she chose very carefully out of countless many.
But Ben, he was the one for her... with all their ups and downs
They settled in the country and she gave away her gowns

Now in her Hunter wellies striding down the riverbank
With Ollie, Ted and I bringing up her flank.
'Come on me darlings,' she hollers..... Stomping off,
'We'll walk to Guildford lock and Ollie please don't cough.'

We'll warn of noises she can't hear and defend her to the core,
And let her rest a while when her eye is very sore.
And when her knees go clickity clack we'll make a little joke
About her gnashers (in the glass) which she put in to soak.

Canine Fahionata's

We're going to smarten up a bit; we're down in the dumps,
After a bleak and dreary winter Teddy's got the grumps...
A blow-dry and trim's not needed, 'Thank goodness' Ollie cries,
'But something has to cheer us', says Ted, rolling his eyes.

Let's go to the new Pet Market - that should cheer us up,
'Good idea Dolly', squeals Ted, (like a new born pup).
Ollie's unenthusiastic; he's too old for jaunts and japes,
So it's agreed he can stay home and nibble on Doggie Shapes.

The market takes our breath away; it's full of everything,
There are rabbits, mice and parrots and books on ferreting.
Guinea pigs and chinchillas and snakes that shed their skins,
Cute kittens and aquariums and fish with silver fins.

Teddy's rapt and captivated standing just inside the door,
He's never seen a hamster or any such thing before.
But Mummy steers us gently towards the 'Pet Boutique'
Where there's designer gear, panache and very chic.

My choice is very femme fatale and so this season's Prada,
But Ted hates all this fussiness, (He fancies enchilada).
So Mummy chooses red for him and blue for Oliver,
(The blue will look so pretty against his pale white fur).

Ted wants some piggy ears and I need dental sticks,
Ollie's craving rawhide and I want to see the baby chicks.
I gaze at them in awe – they're so fluffy and kinda nice,
Ted says they'd look better in a pan with lots of rice!!

Now we're home and inspecting our new wares
Telling Ollie all about our trip as we trundle up the stairs.
Seeing me in pink Ollie puckers his furrowed brow -
I'm feeling rather nervous, 'Do I look like an over-dressed cow'?

Grandma comes to visit; she keeps up with fashion trends,
(But sometimes finds it tricky with a tummy that distends).
Her teeth drop in surprise and she hitches up her garters
When she sees such well-dressed canine fashionata's!!

Dearest Sox

Now Ollie asked me to tell about his dear friend Sox
Alas, no longer with us...but in a crimson velvet box.
She was his number one friend for ten years of her life,
Giving such devotion, (in fact Ollie's trouble and strife).

Dear Sox was quite a wanderlust and always on the go,
With her mistress Carolyn they'd drive down to Truro
And sit among the sand dunes sharing a Cornish pasty,
Watching the sea ebb away until their eyes grew misty.

Sox would walk alongside Ollie on the Lammas land,
Chasing the trembling butterflies, oh, but life was grand.
Together they would run and play by the river Wey,
Come rain or shine for ten long years every single day.

Sox would pause an age seeking out the little moles,
With Ollie standing by watching the new born foals.
Dear Ollie loathed the tracking game and so would just pretend,
But Sox was a fine hunter...to this we must commend.

And so in Doggie Heaven our Beloved Sox now dwells.
Poor Carolyn must walk alone over the fields and fells.
A little of Sox was gently scattered in her favourite spot,
On a Cornish sand-dune...where she'd watched the guillemot.

Rio's Bright Idea

We were just talking one day with Rio, no not Ferdinand...
Rio the welsh Cocker Spaniel, (but actually from Ireland).
Well... he was putting together a football team, maybe a five aside.
Suddenly there was great animation... especially from Boxer Clyde.
He fancies himself as a goalie wearing all the protective gear...
But Rio says he's the goalie 'cos it was his blooming idea.

Teddy will be a defender declaring he'll do his best...
But Ollie won't play; he's far too old and gets pains in his chest.
Ellie said she'd participate and use her slippery tactics,
With some reluctance Rio barked, 'We don't want operatics.'
Benji offered to referee and diplomatically preside
And help the team to victory... 'Hear hear barked Boxer Clyde.'

The decision was unanimous who the striker had to be,
It's that daft as a brush Labradoodle... the one they call Alfie.
He fancies himself like mad but he's young, agile and fit,
He'll score the goals alright, it's just he's a bit of a twit.
And we need a manager who'll perform like Harry Redknapp...
I seconded Patch the Greyhound; (He won't take any crap).

He'll sort this rascally team out and with Rio's boisterous help
Will quickly get them trim on a diet of rice and kelp.
Rio admiringly cried, 'Dolly what a good suggestion,
Cripes you're looking well... are you over that infection?'
I always did think Rio a suave and dashing Cocker
Reminding me of... what's his name, you know that sixties rocker?

'Cheer leaders will be needed,' whispered Ted (the flirt).
'Pretty and appealing... not too shy or introvert.'
And so it was decided to elect the very best lookers....
Like little rosy apples, (not over-ripened cookers)!!
Cuties that would shout and cheer and go hip hip whoopee...
No competition then....its Kuji, Nelly and me (Dolly).

Two weeks have now gone by and the training has paid off,
We didn't think we'd make it 'cos Benji caught a cough.
And so we're here today about to play the Four O'clockers,
They're making so much noise Ollie's taken Beta Blockers.
They've some good players, who think they stand a chance,
But that Archie is a rebel and has chronic flatulence!

Now we've won the toss so Clyde kicks the opening shot
Wishing he hadn't eaten that last remaining Winalot.
Teddy scores a goal and does a jig like Peter Crouch...
Then the crowd is hushed as Benji pulls a red card from his pouch,
It's Charlie the opposing captain who's sent off to sit it out...
For swearing at our Ellie and giving her a walloping clout.

Benji blows the final whistle and so ends this game of ball,
Everyone's exhausted and the score is a close call.
At half time it was two-one but at the end it is a draw,
(This score made Alfie cross.... and so stuck in his craw).
A return match is arranged with the valiant Four O'clockers...
And Rio decides to call his team The West Godalming Rockers.

Beverly and Griff

Beverly owns the Bridal Shop in our local town.
Mummy says she's too old to wear a bridal gown,
But should she be invited to a grand wedding event...
A hat will be required – with feathers to complement.
Ted would sport a bow-tie and Ollie a red cravat,
And I would go to town with tulle and ribbons on my hat.

Beverly has a lovely dog, goes by the name of Griff,
His coat is brown and white and he sports a little quiff.
He's just the cutest dog and I love it when we meet...
As he gives all the gossip and makes my day complete.
He loves watching the brides as they squeeze into a ten,
Then appearing saddened when the buttons won't fasten.

'I must go on a diet,' they scream, 'Just look at my hips,'
But Beverly has the answer as she brews some PG Tips.
'We'll take a dart out here and of course remove the bones,
Our seamstress works miracles, so calm yourself Miss Jones,
Your day will be just wonderful and I won't tell a soul
That you're a size fourteen or where you have that little mole.'

Wondrous Secret

I have such a wondrous secret...would you like to know it as well?
I told it to Ollie this morning and I'm quite sure that Ollie won't tell.
Last night I went into the study....nobody knew I was there.....
And I saw the most beautiful baby asleep in a blue pushchair.

Her dress was pale pink organza; I just couldn't resist a peep,
With hair so soft and curly and her dear little eyes were asleep.
I kissed her pretty snub nose, all pink and smelling like honey
And she looked at me out of one eye as if to say, 'Look at me Dolly.'

Then Mummy appeared in the doorway...saying Ssssh! But all in vain,
'She's awake, let me introduce you... my granddaughter Buttercup Jane.
She'll be staying with us for the night 'cos her Mummy's not very well
And I know you'll help me with baby...if she wakes ring this little bell.'

So I sat all night guarding this bundle of joy and sweet happiness....
And this morning Mummy woke her gently... with a kiss and a little caress.
She went home before Teddy and Ollie could see this baby so small
But I kissed her goodbye in her basket.... in the study just off the hall.

As I sit by the fire with my squeaky thinking of Buttercup Jane and me
We'll be friends forever and ever; I just know it is meant to be.
I haven't told Teddy about her...he'll say, 'You've been dreaming again,
Eating that cream cheese last night may just have addled your brain.'

Stanley

Stanley's a Lhasa Apso....
Trying to win a coveted prize,
He's staggeringly good-looking
With gorgeous hazel eyes.
He's scrubbed and disinfected
And severely brushed for fleas,
Now heavy-eyed and nodding
He looks like the bees knees.

He'll re-arrange your furnishings
With dedicated zeal,
Flipping cushions airborne
With a little yappy squeal.
Making puerile barks and growls
Exhibiting whose boss....
A bit like Sir Alan Sugar
When wound up and very cross.

He looks just like our Teddy,
(The image I would say)...
Both are graciously good-natured,
Impish and casually blasé.
Ted's nick-name is 'Dumpling'
While Stanley's is 'Scruff-bag',
Whatever we care to call 'em
Their bums and tails will wag.

The Apso's are amazing....
So affable and wise,
Quick responding and sensitive,
The first to socialise.
The Tibetan monks of long ago
Knew a thing or two...
As Apso's brought them luck,
So to pay for was taboo.

Now the competition's over,
Stanley didn't win a prize,
Couldn't the judges see?
His charm before their eyes.
He wasn't placed at all
Even failed the final ten,
But next year..... If God is willing
He'll do it all again.

How's Your Father?

Ollie and Ted are talking...
Not about hunting or walking
Just a bit of how's your father?
A bit of the other (if you'd rather).

Ollie who's still intact (say),
Has never ever had his day.
He says he hasn't lost his drive...
A bit of the other and he'd thrive.

Once or twice he almost did it
With a doggie known as Poppet.
She was a flighty King Charles spaniel
(Had two pups with a dog called Daniel).

But his days are numbered now,
He foresees his final bow.
His age is showing, that's for sure,
With failing heart, (there is no cure).

He still looks at the pretty bitches,
(Not for him the crabby witches).
In old age he's more pernickety,
Always was picky and finicky.

But his mind is still so young
And this spring has finally sprung,
So on this sunny day in May
Let an old dog have his day.

Bed Time

When it comes to bed-time Teddy's not too bright...
He makes us hang around in the dead of night.
He don't care if it's cold or raining bucket loads,
We have to stand and wait like soggy, sodden toads.

He saunters up and down...Mummy says, 'I'm warning you
I'll catch my death out here and maybe even flu.'
Oliver has his coat on and Mummy has a hood,
If he doesn't do a wee soon we'll get caught in a flood.

Oliver's now quite cross saying, 'Dolly I've had enough,
I'm going home this instant 'cause I've got a chesty cough.'
Now we're all quite anxious and Mummy starts to shout,
'Teddy get a move on....It's a bad night to be out.'

Then we see Ted hover under the old lime tree,
Why should it take so long to do his bed-time wee?
It's really very creepy here with the hooting owls,
The witchy bats are over-head and an old Tom cat meows.

We start to head for home...In this night so wet and black,
Can we make the front door before they all attack?
The badgers and the foxes are lurking in the bush...
I know they're there 'cause I can see and smell the foxy brush.

It's like a horror story going for our late night wee,
Especially as dear Teddy thinks he's out on a jolly.
He doesn't seem to comprehend the dangers all around
As he slowly sniffs and snuffles all along the ground.

Now we're back at the front door, safe and sound again...
And hearing Trevor McDonald reading News at Ten
In such melodious dulcet tones he sends us all to sleep,
With not another word or bark, commotion or a peep.

Little Nelly

To-day we walked with Beverley and Griff along the river Wey,
It was to be a quick walk as the sky was unsettled and grey.
Then we met the tiniest Yorkie, sitting amongst the phlox,
Her name was Little Nelly and she was such a chatter-box!

Ollie was dumfounded to see a dog so minute,
But Ted was quite smitten and thought she was awfully cute.
'Pin back your ears;' she cried 'I've a tale to tell you now.'
She had to shout 'cos nearby a tractor started to plough.

She said, 'twas a slimy toad that leapt and made her panic,
In terror she fled her garden into the heavy mid-day traffic.
Just as the police arrived to rescue Nell from her plight
A juggernaut passed over her, so the future didn't look bright!!

But Nell fled those mammoth tyres and shivering with sheer panic
Managed to escape unscathed her near death.......... so titanic.
Thus running for her life she came upon Loseley's farm,
Hoping she'd find a haven in a warm and cosy barn.

Now a farmyard has many perils, so to ensure Nell came to no harm
A search party was organised down on this infamous farm.
Everything came to a standstill which is dire at harvest time,
But animal welfare is vital (She could've dropped into the lime).

By now Nelly's owner was howling, causing chaos and mayhem,
Crying so much for Nell that she choked and gagged on her phlegm.
Hearing this heart-rending tale poor Ted was starting to whimper,
'He cries all the time at sad stories,' shouted Ollie losing his temper.

Ted, feeling moved by this tale gave Little Nelly a kiss,
Shocked she fell down the bank and a swan lobbed her back with a hiss.
Poor Little Nell gave a trembled shiver to regain her calm composure,
While Teddy primped and preened (again) just like an Apso poseur.

'What happened next?' Cried Griff wiping his anxious brow -
'Well, 'twas old Bert who found me sitting with the Hampshire sow'
'Now what 'ave we 'ere?' Bert asked, gently putting her under his arm.
She mimicked old Bert to a tee and Ted saw she had oodles of charm.

Thank God there's a happy ending and Little Nell was escorted home.
'Let this be a lesson to you all,' she declared... 'don't ever wander or roam.'
We listened in awe to Nell and we miss her... since she moved to the coast,
But spare a thought for the Hampshire sow, 'cos now he's your Sunday roast!

Fat Teddy

We're bewailing Teddy to lose a bit of weight,
It's such an effort now to shove him through the gate.
Mummy calls him Dumpling, (to shame and disgrace)
But all to no avail, he still stuffs his little face.

Gobbling everything in sight and causing a furore,
He's like a Dyson Cleaner - vacuuming the floor.
With every morsel sticking to his face of furry Velcro,
In desperation Mummy screams, 'Is he still on appro'?

Waiting for toasty crusts to be cut at breakfast–time,
Then dunking them in jams of oranges and lime.
(We regularly threaten him with the doggy army)
As he begs for French bread and lovely smoked pastrami

With a fine-tuned ear for the opening of a packet,
Even pastille paper rustling in Mummy's jacket.
He begs for England when it's lamb or rib of beef,
(We threaten deportation to the Great Barrier Reef)!

Tea-time is a nightmare for guests that come to call...
They have to eat their biscuits standing in the hall.
He'll do somersaults galore for a Jammy Dodger,
Chocolate fudge, Macaroons even a Jolly Roger.

We love him dearly but now he's sixteen kilos -
The time has come to hide his treat of milky Cheerios.
He'll be portion controlled and fed on lovely coley,
Mummy won't stand for his bunkum and baloney

There'll be no chocolate cake or sugar coated treats
And Lord help him if he bamboozles, tricks or cheats.
If the worse comes to the worse we'll use a rubber band
To knot round his tummy, (I'm sure he'll understand).

So yes he's eating coley and cod with some brown rice
And yes he's eating cabbage which he thinks is rather nice.
And yes he's getting slimmer but still frequently weighed
To maintain his beauty of which we're all amazed.

Buttercup Jane

'Twas Buttercup Jane's first birthday
And we were all invited for tea.
There was a mass of people
And of course, Teddy and me.
Dear Ollie stayed at home
He was not too well that day.
(His cough's getting worse and
Now blind he cannot play).

We were told to mind our manners
By Ollie before we left home.
And Mummy brushed Ted's tail
And gave his beard a comb.
We had the birthday presents
And a card with a birthday wish,
Bought in a shop called 'Pavilion'
And wrapped by that nice lady Trish.

Oh! Buttercup Jane was excited...
She chuckled and giggled with glee.
And her little pink fists were out-stretched
And beckoned to Teddy and me.
In an instant she was up on her feet,
'Her first step,'.......... everyone cried!
Then just as quickly she fell,
With a bump....and everyone sighed.

She had some lovely presents....
Like Sooty with a magic wand,
And Granny bought animal books
And a National Savings Bond.
She had so many presents
From those who love her most.
And then the champagne popped,
And the grown-ups drank a toast.

We watched in awe as Buttercup Jane
Threw balloons in the air.
With her face covered in birthday cake
And jam stuck like glue to her hair.
She'd tried to push a cheese straw....
Up her little nose.
And pineapple jelly ended up....
In between her toes.

By the time the food was scoffed,
And flutes of champagne drank,
Buttercup Jane had fallen asleep
In the arms of her uncle Frank.
Who'd crooned a baby's lullaby...
Whilst rocking to and fro,
And *everyone* dropped off to sleep
For half an hour or so.

Then someone started snoring
And everyone woke up.
Granny had indigestion
And delivered a loud hiccup
Someone said, 'It's cold in here!'
So the fire was turned on....
And someone else made coffee,
(And Teddy ate a scone).

We got home at around six o'clock,
(With birthday cake for Ollie)...
He said he was feeling better
But still a bit wibbly wobbly.
Mummy was very tired...
So she had her meal on a tray.
And we all went to bed very early
After such an exciting day.

The Diet

I have an itchy skin condition,
(And it's flared up again).
I'm on a rigorous diet
To alleviate the pain.

It's hypo allergenic...
Mummy insists I eat it all.
Six months I must endure it
Well.... things have gone to the wall.

Jane (the vet) says, 'To conquer the itching
Eliminate all fresh foods...
Just give her one flavour of biscuit,
It might even improve her moods'.

Now I like Jane a lot (you know),
But this is going too far!
I'll lose all my personality...
Please give me some food from a jar.

I used to have lovely boiled chicken,
Cooked in vegetable stock.
Then there was sumptuous pot roast
With vegetables tossed in a wok.

So now I'm sad and dejected
And I might leave home in a huff,
If I don't get a good meal at dinner
I guess I'll be packing my stuff!!

Reveille

I awoke this morning... snuggled close to Ted,
Nose to nose together on Mummy's king-size bed,
Little snorey murmurings emanated from his nose,
And a whiff of last night's chicken stew(Ugh)!....I suppose.

I watched his charismatic features pucker at the dawn.
With an impulsive shudder he gave a shiver and a yawn
Making his whiskers tickle... like a brush against my eyes
As he opened his to meet mine... in breath-taking surprise.

Mummy was still fast asleep - (I thought we'd over-slept),
So I woke her up with kisses.... at that I'm quite adept.
And she always says the same thing, 'Hello sweetie-pie.'
Before pulling back the curtains to see if it's wet or dry.

Dearest Ollie is now very old and has a dicky heart
And so needs waking gently to give him a head start.
(It's a blessing if his shaky legs can hold his body up.....
So we coax and coerce him like a little month old pup)!

Teddy tumbled down the stairs to wait at the front door
As dear Ollie took his tablets... a now twice daily chore.
I was snug beneath the duvet...... until the very last minute....
When Mummy shouted, 'Dolly Gee you really are the limit.'

I scurried down the stairs to, 'Well, here she is at last....
Now shall we have our walk first or do you want breakfast?'
We're like a troop of soldiers being kitted out by Mum.....
'Now have you got your poo bags and where's my chewing gum?'

It's a minute to the river.... through the old lock gates,
There we stood and scanned the path looking for our mates.
Ollie slowly walked with Mummy ...on the lead of course
While Ted and I ran on ahead ...through the prickly gorse.

We met Patch and Lola but they couldn't stop to play
But coming up behind them was Benji.... going our way.
Soon a pack had gathered with Alfie, Ellie and Mops
Then Rio appeared....... with sand all round his chops!

'Twas when we reached the meadow that the fun began...
We met a huge Newfoundland by the name of Aga Khan.
He was so big he couldn't run as fast as Ted or me....
So we played a little hide and seek behind the Maple tree.

Our walk was nearly over.......Ollie was feeling tired
And a rainstorm was looming so a brolli was required.
We jostled through the kissing gate into Catteshall Lane...
And this afternoon with luck.............. we'll do it all again.

Kuji's Birthday

The barbeque was spitting, such aroma's filled the air
Of little chicken drumsticks...for all of us to share.
'Twas mouth-wateringly delicious to say the very least.
'Twas Kuji's garden party..........a Happy Birthday feast.

Dear Ollie had a cuppa and a Rich Tea as his treat,
His teeth are very fragile so cannot manage meat.
Teddy scoffed the choccy drops dunked in pink ice-cream,
Not that we were counting but he must have had fourteen.

Hearing the adults chatting about oh! This and that...
Mainly trivial gossip, who's lost weight and who's got fat.
'Have another glass of wine, forget the calories...
The garden is enchanting, did you grow those peonies?'

Now Mummy's got her camera but Kuji won't say cheese.
'Come on stand close together......try saying strawberries.'
At last................... we were settled in regimented file,
The camera clicked its shutter.......but I forgot to smile.

Ted was really naughty 'cos he found the compost heap
And decided after all that grub to have a little sleep.
Mummy was enraged when he appeared with worms and peel
All around and up his nose........organically surreal.

Everyone sang 'Happy Birthday' and ate some strawberry cake,
Then we took a stroll around Broadwater Lake.
We met Alfie and Jet and a Basset down from Pinner...
And to everyone's surprise Teddy asked, 'What's for my dinner?'

I'm Sorry

I'm lying in my basket
Not feeling very well.
I haven't been on par,
In fact I feel like hell.
I couldn't go this morning,
I couldn't go at lunch,
I couldn't go this evening
And now I have a hunch...
That I might go after hours,
At least that's what I think,
'Cos my tummy's got a rumble
And I think it's on the blink.

Now everyone's in bed...
What am I going to do?
Mummy's sleeping soundly
And I really need to pooh.
My tummy's still rumbling...
It's churning all the more
I can't wait till morning
So I'll go at the front door.
Oh Mummy, I'm so sorry!
I didn't know what to do,
But now I'm feeling better...
Do you think it was the stew?

Toby and Fred

Toby....... is Mummy's young grandson
(He's caring and alert).
Who dreams of playing football
In the Chelsea shirt.
He'll be picked to play for England
On the hallowed turf,
When he's a little bit older......
And stopped playing with his smurf.

We'll watch from the VIP's lounge,
(At maybe Wembley Park).
As Toby scores to win
We'll gesticulate and bark.
And when the Queen presents the cup
Into Toby's tremulous hands....
There'll be adulation on the pitch
And pandemonium in the stands.

Happiness he says, is ninety minutes
(On a pitch).
A stadium of loyal, devoted fans
And Roman Ambromovitch.
But in the meantime,
There's homework to be done,
And his chores..... to earn him money
For that Star Trek laser gun.

Fred....... is Toby's wire Dachshund,
(A lazy little hound).
Who doesn't enjoy walking
And barks at every sound.
He surveys his canine kingdom.....
From a very old grungy armchair,
Like Nero the great roman emperor
Or even Tony Blair.

No-one can sit on Fred's grungy chair,
(Just a minion or two).
It used to belong to a three piece suite,
When spotless, hairless and new.
But now the room's being re-furbished
And Fred's chair is not in the great plan
So he's having a strike called a 'Sit-in'....
As only dear Freddy can.

Now Toby and Fred are the same age,
(Around December time).
They'll stuff themselves on turkey
While guzzling coke with lime.
And gifts will be wrapped and presented,
And crackers pulled in glee,
And never will such celebrations...
Be seen since the Queen's jubilee.

Gastro What?

I've got the colly-wobbles and I don't feel well at all,
I can't eat my breakfast or play with my blue ball.
Mummy's hovering over me...she knows something's wrong
As she tries to dress quickly, (She's still in her sarong).

I've been sick in the kitchen, the bed-room and the hall,
In fact all around the house and even up the wall.
Mummy's apprehensive...her voice an octave raised
Says, she's got to ring the vet and won't be deterred or fazed.

Hence I'm sitting in the vets with trembly jolts and jerks,
Everyone is fussing...even the admin clerks.
The vet feels round my tummy and I shed a little tear
Especially when he sticks that thing right up my rear.

'She's in some discomfort,' he says with sympathy.
'It's gastroenteritis, so no lunch, treats or tea.
I'm wrapped up in my blanket snuggled next to Mum,
Hoping that this abstinence will cure my aching tum.

Teddy says, 'What's wrong? You look peculiar and ill.
And what's this gastrowotsit, do you have to take a pill?'
Now I'm not a spiteful dog but Ted does go on and on,
And this gastrothingymebob makes me crotchety and wan.

I'm taking herbal tablets and swigging God knows what
'Cause one minute I'm cold and then I'm boiling hot.
But Mummy says, 'tomorrow I'll be as right as rain....
I'd better be, 'cos Aunty Kelly's visiting from Bahrain.

Jack the Carpenter's Mate

As far as working dogs go.............Jack is one of a kind,
Working Monday to Friday he doesn't seem to mind.
His vocation is keeping the workshop free of rats and mice,
(Jack can catch 'em faster than you can throw a dice).
From the corner of his eye he'll watch the cabinet-maker
Restoring furniture by Adam, Kent and Shaker.
Jack loves the rich aromas of satinwood and yew,
Sniffing the sawdust from beech and chestnut too.
And lime wood.... used by Master Grinling Gibbons,
Famous for carving birds, intricate lace and ribbons.
Chairs by Hepplewhite or perhaps a 'farthingale,'
With swirls and curvy edges in the style of Chippendale.
And bookcases and consoles, mahogany inlaid
Are lovingly refurbished here for the antique trade.

Jack's favourite place to sit is on a spoon-back chair,
Upholstered in gold satin (and covered in Jack's hair).
It's been there for many years and beyond restoration,
The upholstery is frayed and the frame has infestation.
He sits upon this little chair surveying the workforce,
Listening to lathes turn and the humorous discourse.
Occasionally watching Ned searching for woodworm,
And finding some will tut and click his dentures to affirm!
Being in this environment he's picked up quite a knack
For history and fine art..........this clever little Jack.
Listening to the joiners as they discuss with pleasure,
The latest chair to be restored......a Louis fifteenth treasure.

But most of all he knows on the dot of half past four
His master will be ready to lock the workroom door!

More 'Waggy Tail's by the Wey

Alas, it's time to say good-bye and I'm full of sorrow
But first let me mention the pals I'll see tomorrow......

Pearl, a Border terrier who makes a fuss of me,
She jogs twice a day, and is as fit as a hungry flea.

We'll see Ted's admirer...a bouncy Spaniel, Jazz....
He's full of curiosity, awareness and pizzazz.

And Dougal the Tibetan, full of feel-good cheer,
Like an express train coming at you from the rear.

Rolly the sweet Dachshund who always makes us titter
As he hops, skips and jumps to get a little fitter.

There's Scooter the Jack Russell with his owner Ann
And Madeline the well-groomed silken-haired Afghan.

The Newfoundland, 'Purdy' named after a hair-do....
As worn by Joanna Lumley to name but just a few.

We meet Daisy and Oscar to discuss the Daily News...
You know... general gossip, who's *not* picked up their poos?

There's Dave the Great Dane, he's still just a pup.....
But wouldn't look unbefitting winning, 'The Queen's Gold Cup.'

And so my story ends and I'll leave you with a sigh
Maybe we'll meet tomorrow.............till then I'll say goodbye.

Printed in the United States
1480LVUK00005B